Wolves

A Predatory Fairy Tale

Steve Yockey

A SAMUEL FRENCH ACTING EDITION

SAMUEL FRENCH

FOUNDED 1830

SAMUELFRENCH.COM
SAMUELFRENCH-LONDON.CO.UK

FOR PRODUCTION ENQUIRIES

UNITED STATES AND CANADA

Info@SamuelFrench.com

1-866-598-8449

UNITED KINGDOM AND EUROPE

Plays@SamuelFrench-London.co.uk

020-7255-4302

Each title is subject to availability from Samuel French, depending upon country of performance. Please be aware that *WOLVES* may not be licensed by Samuel French in your territory. Professional and amateur producers should contact the nearest Samuel French office or licensing partner to verify availability.

MUSIC USE NOTE

Licensees are solely responsible for obtaining formal written permission from copyright owners to use copyrighted music in the performance of this play and are strongly cautioned to do so. If no such permission is obtained by the licensee, then the licensee must use only original music that the licensee owns and controls. Licensees are solely responsible and liable for all music clearances and shall indemnify the copyright owners of the play(s) and their licensing agent, Samuel French, against any costs, expenses, losses and liabilities arising from the use of music by licensees. Please contact the appropriate music licensing authority in your territory for the rights to any incidental music.

IMPORTANT BILLING AND CREDIT REQUIREMENTS

If you have obtained performance rights to this title, please refer to your licensing agreement for important billing and credit requirements.

WOLVES opened as part of a rolling world premiere with support from the National New Play Network's Continued Life of New Plays Fund on November10, 2012 at the King Plow Arts Center in Atlanta, GA. The play was produced by Actor's Express Theatre Company with Artistic Director Freddie Ashley and Managing Director Nan Barnett. The Director was Melissa Foulger with scenic design by Seamus M. Bourne, lighting design by Benn Tilley, sound design by Dan Bauman, costume design by Jonida Beqo, and prop design by Lindsay Moore. The cast was as follows:

BEN	Clifton Guterman
JACK	Brian E. Crawford
WOLF	Joe Sykes
NARRATOR	Kate Donadio

WOLVES opened as part of a rolling world premiere with support from the National New Play Network's Continued Life of New Plays Fund on November 15, 2012 at the Den of Muses in New Orleans, LA. The play was produced by Southern Rep with Producing Artistic Director Aimee Hayes. The Director was Aimee Hayes with scenic and prop design by Elizabeth Harwood, lighting design by Amanda Woods, and sound design by Mike Harkins. the cast was as follows:

BEN	Andrew Farrier
JACK	Taylor McLellan
WOLF	Benjamin Carbo
NARRATOR	Kerry J. Cahill

WOLVES opened as part of a rolling world premiere with support from the National New Play Network's Continued Life of New Plays Fund on November 30, 2012 at the Tempe Canter for the Performing Arts in Tempe, AZ. The play was produced by Stray Cat Theatre Company with Artistic Director Ron May. The Director was Ron May with scenic design by Eric Beeck, lighting by Ellen Bone, sound design by Joey Trahan, costume design Danny Chihuahua, and prop design by Kelly Coughlin-Celaya. The cast was as follows:

BEN	Tyler Eglen
JACK	Samuel E. Wilkes
WOLF	Adam Pinti
NARRATOR	Yolanda London

WOLVES opened as part of a rolling world premiere with support from the National New Play Network's Continued Life of New Plays Fund on March 8, 2012 at Celebration Theatre in Los Angeles, CA with Artistic Directors Michael Matthews & Michael A. Shepperd and Executive Director Michael Kricfalusi. The Director was Michael Matthews with scenic design by Kaitlyn Pietras, lighting design by Timothy Swiss, sound design by Cricket Myers, and costume and prop design by Michael O'Hara. The cast was as follows:

BEN . . . . Nathan Mohebbi

JACK . . . . Matthew Magnusson

WOLF . . . . Andrew Crabtree

NARRATOR . . . . Katherine Skelton

CHARACTERS

NARRATOR – A woman with a warm, soothing voice and a quirky sense
of humor; she's definitely your friend. At least she wants you to
believe that. Strong and put together, she's also clearly in charge
here. In a form fitting skirt and blouse, her hair up, high heels.

BEN – A young man, managing to look innocent and pretty together in
spite of deep delusional psychosis and a crippling unrequited love.
He covers well until he can't. Barefoot, bed-head, in jeans and a
v-neck white t-shirt.

JACK – A young man, pretty, cocky, thinks he knows better, but out of
place and a little too willing to believe; thus, starting to see things.
But fighting it. In a fitted dark polo shirt & tight jeans, dressed for
a date.

WOLF – A man, muscular, physical, a but scruffy, a guy's guy. Casual,
amiable, charm with hint of sorrow. But it's more in what he says
not how he says it. In a tight, graphic print t-shirt & Levis sporting a
dark blue bandana in his back left pocket.

NOTES ON STAGING

[ ] indicate overlapping dialogue.

The visible floor plan of the apartment (including the entrance hall,
living room, a small bathroom and Ben's bedroom) is taped out on the
floor of the space with white tape. There are no walls, but the tape is
recognized as such.

An idea of the floor plan is included at the back of the book – something
of a jumping off point.

The items specified in each area should be the only items on stage.

The lighting, while lower on the whole, moves from something warm to
something colder and harsher as the play progresses.

I. Safe & Sound

*(The **NARRATOR** sits on her stool off to one side of the stage. An inconspicuous tin bucket is near one of the stool legs but out of the way. **BEN** sits at the **NARRATOR**'s feet with a guitar. They are warmly illuminated.)*

*(As the audience enters, **BEN** plays the guitar and sings with the **NARRATOR** – a gentle, harmonized and private thing. It has the feel of a casual jam session and they enjoy each other's company. Stripped down versions of songs* like: "Unravel" by Bjork; "Change of Heart" by El Perro Del Mar; "Hysteric" by Yeah Yeah Yeahs; "A&E" by Goldfrapp; "Peach, Plum, Pear" by Joanna Newsom; "My Body is a Cage" by Arcade Fire; and "Crystalize" by The XX.)*

*(Once the houselights go down, the music continues. Eventually, the **NARRATOR** stops singing, but **BEN** continues on with the guitar, singing softly to himself now. He keeps plucking at the guitar and looks up to her.)*

BEN. I'm listening to music right now.

NARRATOR. Yes.

BEN. I'm listening to music in my room.

NARRATOR. Yes, that's right.

BEN. But I'm singing with you.

NARRATOR. Oh, I so love when we sing together.

BEN. Me too, I do too.

NARRATOR. It just works, doesn't it?

BEN. And it takes my mind off things.

---

*Please see Music Use Note on page 3.

NARRATOR. That's so true.

BEN. I can always count on you.

NARRATOR. No matter how bad things get.

BEN. Oh… Okay.

NARRATOR. But they're not that bad.

BEN. Right.

NARRATOR. In here at least.

BEN. Okay, yes. In here. Just don't…

(He stops playing the guitar.)

Don't tell me anything bad, okay?

NARRATOR. Ben, I only tell you the things you need to know.

BEN. Sometimes it's scary, it scares me.

NARRATOR. Sometimes it should, but…you're safe right now.

BEN. Yes.

NARRATOR. In here.

BEN. Because this is a safe place.

NARRATOR. Yes.

BEN. Good.

NARRATOR. Until you start to think it's not.

BEN. See, that's what I'm, that's kind of ominous.

NARRATOR. It's not ominous, Ben. It's foreboding.

BEN. What does [that mean?]

NARRATOR. [Shhhh.] Safe and sound.

(He looks at her. She smiles.)

BEN. Okay. Okay, safe and sound.

(BEN *begins to play again, singing softly to himself. The* NARRATOR *smiles at him, hops off her stool and takes in the audience. She gives them a nod of acknowledgment. She then turns and presents the space.*)

(*As she does, the lights rise on the rest of the stage. It is relatively bare. But the outline of the front half of a two-bedroom apartment is marked out on the floor in white tape. A hallway comes from the back of the space with a full sized bedroom stage right and a small bathroom stage left. The hallway then opens into a main living room.)*

*(Downstage of the bedroom is a small entry way and the front door. Just down stage and outside of the front door is the **NARRATOR**'s stool. In the living room there is a couch with a small stack of books next to it. In the kitchen there is cart or shelf with several bottles of alcohol and some tumblers.)*

(Next to the front door is a chair with a red hoodie thrown over the back of it. An axe leans against the chair with a small pile of firewood sitting next to it.)

(The bathroom is empty.)

*(In **BEN**'s bedroom, there is a small bed, a stereo system with a pair of oversized headphones attached via a ridiculously long chord. Next to the stereo is a churning lava lamp. This is on for the entire opening sequence and is lit for the entirety of the play, even during blackouts.)*

*(After a moment, the **NARRATOR** turns to the audience again.)*

II. Dark Falls Outside

NARRATOR. Once upon a time, hmmm, you know, I should say up front: this isn't a pretty story or anything. It's a lot of things, but it gets a little messy and I want to be really direct about that, all right? Good. Now, once upon a time…

(She stops and looks at **BEN**. *He is still playing, singing quietly. She signals for the audience to give her a moment, kneels down and whispers something in* **BEN***'s ear. She blocks her mouth and his ear with her hand, something even more private.)*

*(***BEN** *stops playing. His eyes go wide with wonder, then fear, as if he can see something horrible coming. He shakes it off and scrambles down the taped out hallway and into his room. Once there, he sets his guitar on the floor, sits down next to an old stereo system and puts on an oversized pair of headphones. He holds them to his ears and listens.)*

(The **NARRATOR** *turns back to the audience.)*

Okay. Once upon a time, there was an intrepid young man. Named Ben.

(She indicates **BEN**.*)*

He moved from a very small town where he didn't fit very well to a very large city where he didn't fit very well. And he didn't know how to handle very well what it means to move from a very small town to a very large city. Some people don't know how to be alone. Ah, and some people don't know that they don't know how to be alone until they're suddenly. All. Alone. And Ben was one of those people. So the city became more menacing day by day. Became more crowded, more isolating, as it does for some people sometimes. But for Ben, specifically, the city grew into an entirely different kind of place. A place that filled his eyes and made his heart race with fear, a place full of the darkest nights, a creeping pitch black filled with dangerous animals, hidden threats, a place that spilled out of his head and anxiously became the world around him. It was a horrible way to exist. All. Alone.

But fortunately for Ben, he stumbled upon an ally of sorts. So he was lucky. Maybe. And he learned how to be alone with someone else. Which sounds worse than it is. But that's what he did; he fell in love with Jack.

(*JACK carefully, quietly makes his way down the hall, hugging the wall across from* **BEN***'s room. He darts past* **BEN***'s door and makes his way to his shoes, sitting just inside the front door.* **BEN** *takes off the headphones.*)

But the sad fact is that kind of love isn't really love, it's just need, so the two young men soon fell out of love. Or out of the idea of love and into something else. But because that need between them was so strong, the young men tried to still be something to each other, as happens for some people sometimes.

(*As* **JACK** *is putting on his shoes, The* **NARRATOR** *casually knocks a book or two off the pile and onto the floor.* **JACK** *flinches and hurries to get his shoes on.* **BEN** *hears the books fall, gets up in his room, sets down the headphones and makes his way into the hall.*)

And that thing, as mentioned, was being alone, together, in a very small apartment in a very large city.

(**BEN** *sees* **JACK***, stops, heads through the living room and begins looking through the stack of books.*)

BEN. Hey Jack.

(*JACK is startled.*)

JACK. I thought you were listening to music.

BEN. Uh huh.

JACK. Something depressing probably.

BEN. Have you seen that stack of menus? I was thinking we could order some Chinese food tonight, if they're still delivering.

JACK. Ugh, I don't think eating that Orange Chicken every night really counts as eating Chinese food.

BEN. Why not?

JACK. Because it's a made up thing. It's marketing, Ben, all right? They didn't use to have Orange Chicken. No Chinese peasant ever made Orange Chicken and now it's everywhere.

BEN. You used to love that place.

JACK. Whatever.

BEN. And it tastes good.

JACK. Blah.

BEN. So I don't care if it's pretend. Plus, it makes me feel all Zen-like when I crack open my little fortune cookie. Last time my fortune thing said: "An empty bird cage means freedom."

JACK. Unless they use the bird to make Orange Chicken.

BEN. I guess it's a "glass half full" kinda' thing.

JACK. Well, I'm done with that place. The rice is always over-cooked.

BEN. You're finicky, that's your [problem.]

JACK. [Oh, and my] last fortune cookie said something like, "The world does not change, you do." That's not a fortune, that's some bullshit truism with lottery numbers printed on the back.

(He finds the menus.)

BEN. Better luck tonight maybe.

JACK. Don't want any, thanks.

BEN. Well, then we can order from somewhere else, you pick.

(JACK finishes putting on his shoes.)

JACK. Not really hungry.

BEN. Okay, then did you want to watch a movie or something? I can break open my Kubrick box set, I don't know though, that might be kind of serious.

JACK. Nah.

BEN. Well, I'm running out of ideas, what do you want to do?

JACK. I'm going out.

*(The **NARRATOR** claps once, interrupting and freezing the scene in tableau.)*

NARRATOR. It's also not a regular, lesson-learned kind of story. That just occurred to me to share, just now. As we move along, you probably shouldn't go looking for a moral. You'd be hard pressed to reconcile a moral with this story. Keep that in mind. And listen, if you do happen to stumble across a moral, well then this story is probably closer to you than you'd think and I'm not sure you'll like that very much in the end.

(She laughs.)

Okay? Good. So just then, right then, as the words left Jack's lips, Ben's heart stopped in his chest. Really, it did. And Jack knew that it would, but he just couldn't get out of the apartment fast enough. He's terrible at getting away with things and excellent at getting caught.

(Everything begins moving again.)

BEN. What?

JACK. You heard me, I'm going out.

BEN. It's too late; it's too dark.

(Grabbing the red hoodie off the chair and putting it on.)

JACK. I'm a big boy.

BEN. You're not going [out, okay?]

JACK. [Does this have] to be a thing every single time?

BEN. Uh, don't be stupid.

JACK. Don't call me stupid.

BEN. I'm calling you stupid because that's what people call other people when they're being stupid.

JACK. Very nice.

BEN. No, it's not nice. And I'm not gonna try to call it some nicer thing for you, okay, like naïve? Because you're not naïve, we both know how dangerous it is out there, especially at night, so that just makes you stupid.

JACK. I'm only going to a bar around the corner.

BEN. Why?

JACK. Are you okay?

BEN. I'm fine.

JACK. Don't freak out.

BEN. I'm fine.

JACK. You've kind of got that "freak out" look.

BEN. What does that even, no I don't.

JACK. Like when you attacked the landlord with a screwdriver [and tried to…]

BEN. [Whoa, whoa,] whoa, I did not attack the landlord with a screwdriver. I had a screwdriver in my hand and I may have inadvertently "threatened" the landlord with it.

JACK. Listen, I thought it was funny, but if I hadn't walked in when [I did…]

BEN. [Come on, it's] not like I would have stabbed him.

*(The **NARRATOR** claps once, interrupting and freezing the scene in tableau.)*

NARRATOR. Just want to quickly interject here. He would have. Let me be absolutely clear on this: Ben would have stabbed the landlord with a screwdriver.

(Everything begins moving again.)

JACK. You absolutely would have stabbed him.

BEN. What kind of person stabs someone with a screwdriver?

JACK. You.

BEN. Is that what we're doing? Bringing up potential mistakes from our pasts? Because I don't think you'd like that game.

JACK. I would like it fine, and that's not nice by the way, but we're not bringing up potential mistakes from our past. We're talking about how you tend to freak out and I'm being generous by calling [it that.]

BEN. [He scared] me. He has to tell us before he just comes in here. Anyone would have reacted that way, so that doesn't count.

(JACK chuckles.)

JACK. It's lucky we're still allowed to live here.

BEN. You're luck we're still allowed to live here.

JACK. Fine, we're both lucky. And we've now established you did not and will not go gung ho with a screwdriver on anyone? Great. So then you're fine and I'll see you later.

BEN. Okay. Fine, but [remember…]

JACK. [Oh my god.]

BEN. You know when it gets dark, some people will, not even people, animals, there are animals [that will…]

JACK. [Animals?]

BEN. What?

JACK. You're doing it again.

BEN. No.

JACK. Good. See you later.

BEN. You're going alone?

JACK. You see anyone else?

BEN. That is so incredibly…

(He launches to the front door, but stops himself, centers and recalibrates.)

That doesn't sound like the best plan.

JACK. Ben, move.

BEN. No.

JACK. Okay, if you're gonna', let me frame this for you so you can relax and enjoy your night in without worrying. Why don't you just…just think of it as hunting.

(JACK smiles at him, proud.)

BEN. What?

JACK. I'm going hunting.

BEN. That's not funny.

JACK. It's not supposed to be funny; I'm not trying to be funny. Hunters don't have to be afraid of "animals." So you don't have to worry.

BEN. Well that's just genius. Where's your gun?

JACK. Ben.

BEN. Hunter's don't have to be afraid because they [have guns.]

JACK. [Just because] you say it's scary in the dark, just because you say it over and over again, ad nauseum, doesn't mean I [have to…]

BEN. ["Ad nauseum?"] Where'd you pick [that up?]

JACK. [Doesn't mean] I have to listen to you and stop trying to [pick a fight]

BEN. [You have no idea] what you're inviting in here when you go out there looking for trouble.

JACK. Into the city.

BEN. The forest.

JACK. The big, dark forest.

BEN. Yes.

JACK. I'm not worried.

(JACK *steps into him. Very close. He knows what he's doing.*)

You'll keep me safe, right?

(pause)

BEN. Yes.

JACK. Yes?

BEN. You know I will.

JACK. So…

BEN. Don't do that.

(JACK *breaks away with a smile, zipping up the hoodie.*)

JACK. So then everything's fine.

BEN. We, we don't have to watch Kubrik, we don't have to order Chinese food, we don't have to do anything, okay? As long as we don't do that anything in here.

JACK. That sounds like an amazing evening.

BEN. I can protect you here, but if you're out there by yourself, [at night…]

JACK. [With a] screwdriver?

BEN. I told you, that was [an isolated…]

JACK. [Ben, I don't] actually need you to protect me, physically, it's [not like….]

BEN. [You just] got done [saying that…]

JACK. [You're] getting pretty worked up.

BEN. No.

JACK. I'm not trying to, look… I appreciate you giving me a place to live and [all, but…]

BEN. [This doesn't] have anything to do with that.

JACK. You said you were okay with living together.

BEN. What? I am.

JACK. If you can't handle this, if it's like a jealousy thing, I mean, if it's making you start to go crazy again, [if it's…]

BEN. [Can we] not call it that? You know I don't, it wasn't crazy, it wasn't freaking out, it was just a "rough time" and I'm fine.

JACK. "Animals." You said that.

BEN. "Hunting." You said that.

JACK. Sometimes it's just easier to go along with your, whatever it is, than try to navigate my way back out of it.

BEN. That sounds slippery.

JACK. Tell me about it.

BEN. I didn't mean slippery, I meant dishonest.

JACK. Tell me bout it.

BEN. And you don't have to navigate anything.

JACK. I'm doing it right now, it's happening right now.

BEN. Okay, just stop thinking that I'm jealous or that I'm trying to keep you away from, look, we've done this already, okay? It didn't work out between us, or whatever, but that's how things happen and it's better this way and I get that, I totally get that, this doesn't have anything to do with you living here. I'd rather you live here than be out on the street somewhere.

JACK. I wouldn't be on the street.

BEN. Huh, no, right, I know where you'd be.

JACK. Now what does that mean?

BEN. Nothing.

JACK. Good.

BEN. Just…you never had a hard time finding a bed.

JACK. So I have to kind of pretend that you're not calling me a whore so I don't just punch you in the face. Most nights I'm here, almost every night. Not that it's any [of your…]

BEN. [I don't think] that [about you.]

JACK. [And it's a] little confusing to me when you say you care so much and want me to be okay, everything's great, and then you just start shredding away at me whenever I don't want go along [with…]

BEN. [I'm] sorry.

JACK. I just want to go out for a little bit.

BEN. Maybe, and I'm saying maybe, maybe I get a little jealous still, which I'm handling. Sorry. But I'm not wrong about going out at night. And I'm not crazy.

JACK. I didn't mean "crazy," okay.

BEN. Thank you. And we both know the forest is too dangerous at [night.]

JACK. [But then] you say something crazy.

BEN. I know you see it too, the forest, the way it's not a city, the way it's [full of…]

JACK. [Sometimes.]

BEN. You say you do, you said you do.

JACK. I said a lot of things.

BEN. Oh. Perfect.

JACK. Just, I didn't use to see it at all, but you stay on me about it so much, like you're in my head, so now sometimes I see out there the way you do. But I don't want to, Ben. I don't want to see the world like that. So the rest of the time [it looks…]

BEN. [It doesn't] change.

JACK. It does for me. And it can look different for you, too. I'm not even being all "new agey" about it. If you ever wanna be happy, you have to start making yourself see it differently.

BEN. "The world does not change, you do."

JACK. You think quoting a fucking fortune cookie back to me is gonna help your case?

BEN. "The world does not change, you do."

JACK. Ben, you don't have to be afraid, or you don't know how to not be afraid so I just want you to be more than afraid. You can be other things too, right?

BEN. I can, I am.

JACK. Prove it.

BEN. That's not, even if we see different things when we look out there, even if that's true, neither of us sees anything that's particularly good or that has been particularly good to us. If we agree on that, then I don't understand.

(*The* **NARRATOR** *claps once, interrupting and freezing the scene in tableau.*)

NARRATOR. This seems like an excellent point to, oh, you know, I won't keep doing this. Interrupting. I will, but not this often. However, what I said earlier may have been a bit misleading. Moving from a very small town to a very large city certainly took its toll on Ben. That's true. On Ben's idea of himself and his idea of the city, his idea of himself in the city, all of that, but he could have overcome it. Maybe. Sadly, as is sometimes the case, Ben turned in desperation to other people for comfort. And when I say other people what you should hear is "men." And when I say comfort what you should hear is "love." Both of these things a very big city, the idea of a very big city, would seem to promise in abundance. But what he also found was a healthy disappointment and a fair degree of pain.

(While speaking, she traces the outline of a large heart with her finger over **BEN**'s *heart.)*

Heartbreak, in and of itself, isn't so unusual. People's needs very seldom line up in the right way at the right time, despite volumes of stories to the contrary, stories that paint an overall ideal of how things should work, look, stories that create expectations; thus, heartbreak.

(She touches **BEN**'s *face gently.)*

And one bad fit after the next starts to feel like everyone is a bad fit. And then it starts to feel like someone has to fit, has to be the one. And then? Jack. A young man who was a little too willing to see the world through Ben's eyes and a little too weak to stop when he should have.

(Everything begins moving again as **JACK** *crashes onto the couch and hugs one of the pillows in frustration.)*

JACK. Ben, I'm going stir crazy.

BEN. No, you want to "get off."

JACK. So what? What's wrong with that?

BEN. Nothing.

JACK. What's wrong with me wanting a little bit of affection?

BEN. I said nothing.

JACK. You know that I was sneaking out earlier? Yep. I was really trying hard to sneak out, crept past your room on tiptoe, just so that I wouldn't get trapped in this kind of inquisition.

BEN. Inquisition? It's just a little misunderstanding. I was making all of those suggestions because I didn't realize what you were looking for. So listen…if you're looking for that kind of physical, just, I'm perfectly capable [of giving…]

JACK. [Oh no, stop,] that doesn't work. We tried it and you think it means we're getting back together and we're not getting back [together.]

BEN. [I don't think] that.

JACK. Whenever we're any kind of intimate [now.]

BEN. [Nope.]

JACK. Any kind of physical, yes, you do.

BEN. This is, no, this, you're totally changing the subject, you're trying to make this about us [and I'm…]

JACK. [I can't] stay in here with you every night.

BEN. That's not [what I'm…]

JACK. [Ben, I can't] stay in here with you every night.

BEN. I heard you.

JACK. Then acknowledge it.

BEN. I did, I just did!

　　　(pause)

JACK. Ugh, listen, I don't like when it gets all, you know I care about you. A lot. And we're figuring out how to, okay, it's not like I have to go alone. We used to go out and have fun. You could, you should come out with me?

　　　*(**BEN** just looks at him with something like amazement.)*

When's the last time you went out at night?

BEN. Wolves.

JACK. Stop.

BEN. Wolves.

JACK. Ben.

BEN. I'm sorry if I don't want to get my throat ripped out in a bloody mess while walking [down some…]

JACK. [Ugh, okay,] okay. First off, don't talk like that. Don't
    be morbid. You know I hate blood so the idea of your
    throat being ripped open or out or, I don't wanna'
    picture that. Second, how do you even know that
    wolves would do that?

BEN. Of course they, that's what [wolves do.]

JACK. [How do you] know? Have you ever actually seen a
    wolf, met one, talked to one? How do you know they're
    so bad? How do you know they're even real?

BEN. Listen to you.

JACK. Just because we're afraid of them doesn't mean we
    should be.

BEN. Yes it does.

JACK. Just because some wolves were bad once, doesn't
    mean all wolves are bad.

BEN. Yes it does!

JACK. How do I even get pulled into this over and over,
    fucking wolves. All right, you know what? I'm going
    out. Because I have to even if it is scary or else I won't
    be able to go anymore at all. Like you. So I'm going
    out and I'm going to find you a wolf. Or, no, I'm going
    to find a wolf for me. And maybe he'll be scary. And
    maybe he'll be dangerous. And maybe that's okay
    because it's better than staying in here and slowly
    going crazy with you.

BEN. I'm not crazy; don't [say crazy.]

JACK. [Then whatever's] happening in here; but it feels a
    lot like "crazy."

BEN. Shelter and protection.

JACK. Goodbye.

    (BEN *grabs* JACK *by the arm.*)

    Let go.

BEN. Don't go [out there!]

JACK. [Ben, let] go of me.

BEN. I'm trying to help [you.]

JACK. [What is] wrong with you?

(*JACK pulls free sharply and accidentally hits* **BEN** *in the eye with his arm.* **BEN** *jerks away and then, while holding his hand over one eye, very deliberately looks at* **JACK**.)

BEN. Ow.

(*Pause. Both men are breathing heavy.* **BEN** *sits on the edge of the couch covering his eye.* **JACK** *runs his hand through his hair and calms down. He crosses over to* **BEN**.)

JACK. I'm sorry.

BEN. It's fine; it was an accident.

JACK. It was.

(*JACK reaches out but* **BEN** *knocks his hand away.*)

BEN. Don't touch it.

JACK. I'll get some ice to put [on it.]

BEN. [I thought] you were going out.

JACK. Okay, right.

(*He begins to leave, but* **BEN** *let's out a dramatic sigh as if his eye really hurts.* **JACK** *stops.*)

Ben, you've been great to me and I dig being here, but you need to do a better job of not doing this exact kind of thing. Or I mean, I don't know how long this is sustainable. Something's got to shake you out of it or someone's [got to...]

BEN. [I'm fine.]

JACK. I'm sorry about your eye.

(*The* **NARRATOR** *claps once, interrupting and freezing the scene in tableau. She crosses to* **BEN**, *smiling. She touches just beneath his eye where he was hit.*)

NARRATOR. Does it hurt?

BEN. Not much.

NARRATOR. Don't worry; he'll be back.

BEN. It feels like it's getting worse.

NARRATOR. It only feels that way.

BEN. He never wants to stay.

NARRATOR. And it's so dangerous out there.

BEN. Yes.

NARRATOR. He just doesnt know any better.

BEN. He won't listen.

NARRATOR. He never listens.

BEN. Ever.

NARRATOR. But he'll figure it out eventually, I promise.

BEN. Okay.

NARRATOR. And then it'll all be fine.

BEN. Good.

NARRATOR. If he makes it back in one piece.

BEN. What?

NARRATOR. Shhh. Safe and sound.

> *(She leans in with care and whispers something in his ear, blocking her mouth with her hand. It is a private thing. Light isolates* **BEN** *as he seizes up, becoming very still, and his eyes go wide.)*

> *(The* **NARRATOR** *returns to her stool and* **JACK** *drifts away as the words begin spilling from* **BEN***, like a flood of language, almost religious in its fervor. It begins as a hushed frenzy, so quiet, so still, and becomes something he is not in control of in any way. It physically taxes him, not from the effort but from the speed of the images flashing, the ideas tumbling over each other to get out and become the world around him.)*

BEN. This city isn't safe, this forest, this forest full of towering buildings, trees, buildings, thick trunks, gigantic. They loom. They loom as I walk and I look and they, they block out any kind of light, any kind of anything that could cleanse, they hide the sick, savage secrets that lurk behind their branches, the eyes, hungry animals, in the dark places, it isn't safe at night. They stalk. They stalk when the night falls, heavy and hard. Entire pieces of every street, familiar, vanish into darkness, hushed and horrifying and underneath and dangerous. How can you trust them, the people, the streets, the animals, so hungry, so hungry, and they look at me, like me, they look like anyone, everyone, behind the trees, corners of buildings, roots in sewers that feed these enormous, these enormous, hiding eyes, the teeth, wet and needing, the hunger you can't trust, I can't trust, and he can't, it's only safe in here, small, this place, sound, bright, bright, bright enough to keep the wolves at bay, the dark away, that large dark, so large, so hungry, so vast, so vast, so vast, so vast…

(As he reaches the end of the passage, lights fade on **BEN** *as the distant sounds of howling wind in a vast emptiness rise to consume him. The* **NARRATOR** *remains illuminated dimly along with the lava lamp as lights shift into…)*

III. A Wounded Animal

NARRATOR. Later that same evening…

> *(Lights up on the space. **BEN** sits on his bed next to his stereo, this time with his back to the audience; headphones on, lava lamp churning.)*

> Much later that same evening, in fact, Jack returned to the small apartment. A fifth floor walk-up, by the way, at the very top of the stairwell just below a large, locked door. Nothing on the other side but the dark sky hanging, waiting. And it was probably storming outside, but not in this account. Thunder makes you feel so small, doesnt it? And Jack needed to feel large, brave. To do what he needed to do. To prove what he needed to prove to Ben. And, more urgently, to himself. So for our purposes, the sky was clear. The dark sky he walked under to the bar. Alone. The same sky he walked back under. Less alone. Because Jack had been hunting and it was quite a success.

> *(**JACK** and **WOLF** enter though the front door. They are laughing and **WOLF** is a little bit winded.)*

WOLF. If I lived in a fifth floor walk-up, I'd be miserable.

JACK. You'd be fine.

WOLF. No, it sucks.

JACK. It keeps you in shape.

WOLF. There're lots of ways to stay in shape. I like elevators.

JACK. Well you're up here now.

WOLF. Yes, I am.

JACK. So Wolf, this is the place.

WOLF. Nice.

JACK. Can I take your coat?

> *(**WOLF** takes off his coat and hands it to **JACK**. He hangs it on the coat rack.)*

WOLF. Can I just, why do you keep calling me that? Wolf?

JACK. I don't know.

WOLF. You've been doing it since we left the bar.

JACK. I like it.

WOLF. Little too much to drink.

JACK. Nah.

WOLF. But you know it's not my name, [right?]

JACK. [It's just] a thing I, it's like a little nickname. For tonight. I can stop or whatever.

WOLF. Wolf as in "big bad" [or…?]

JACK. [I just] think it's cute.

WOLF. Is it?

> *(He moves close to* **JACK,** *running his finger across* **JACK***'s chest.)*

Cute?

> *(He lets his palm rest open on* **JACK***'s chest and leans in towards him.* **JACK** *moves away.)*

JACK. Sure.

> *(***WOLF** *laughs to himself, a bit embarrassed.* **BEN** *stands up and then sits back down again, frustrated.)*

WOLF. Well, it's fine by me.

JACK. Can I get you a drink?

WOLF. I was drinking beer at the bar, so if [you…]

JACK. [We] basically have a lot of liquor.

WOLF. We?

JACK. Roommate.

WOLF. Here?

JACK. I'm pretty sure he's in there. He, uh, doesn't go out very much.

WOLF. Ah. I'll just have whatever you're gonna have.

JACK. That works.

> *(***JACK** *fixes two drinks.* **BEN** *hears the men. He moves to put his back against the wall again, eyeing his door suspiciously.)*

WOLF. I gotta, say, I was kinda, surprised. That you, well, that you picked me up. Most guys in that bar don't really talk to me. They see this guy sitting alone, head down, long face, don't look at me like that because I know how I look at that bar. They see this guy and just, well, it's been a while is all.

JACK. You found the darkest corner in there.

WOLF. I'm not a people person.

JACK. What do you mean?

WOLF. It's just something people say, right?

JACK. Okay, I guess, but what does it mean?

WOLF. It's not that I don't like other people, or whatever, I just don't always know how to feel comfortable, that's a shitty, easy word, but okay, I don't know how to be comfortable around other people.

JACK. You mean guys.

WOLF. Sure.

JACK. Huh, then why do you go?

WOLF. Same reason as anyone, I guess.

(As **WOLF** *speaks,* **BEN** *is up and moving, he enters from the bedroom and stands in the hall just at the edge of the living room. He has a black eye.)*

JACK. Oh, Ben, this is my friend from tonight. His name is Wolf.

BEN. Wolf?

WOLF. Okay, that's not my real [name, I'm…]

JACK. [That's what] I'm calling him. I think it fits. Wolf, this is Ben. That is his real name. This is really mostly his place. He's just letting me crash.

WOLF. Nice to meet you.

BEN. Jack, can I talk to you?

JACK. I'm a little busy.

WOLF. What happened to your eye?

*(***BEN** *pulls* **JACK** *aside, but doesn't really whisper.* **JACK** *tries to touch* **BEN***'s eye, but* **BEN** *bats him away.)*

JACK. Ouch, look at your, how is that?

BEN. It hurts.

JACK. It was an accident.

BEN. What are you doing?

JACK. I told you, I went out and [found a...]

BEN. [What stupid thing] are you doing?

JACK. I think we talked about not calling me stupid.

BEN. I think we talked about keeping this place safe.

JACK. *(Quietly...)*

God, just look at him; he's just a guy.

BEN. I see teeth.

JACK. No, you see a guy I brought home. And there's nothing wrong with that.

BEN. You're making a mistake.

JACK. And you're being really rude.

(BEN *stares at* WOLF *as he exits back into his room.* WOLF *finishes his drink and nods with a smile to* BEN. *Once in his room,* BEN *paces for a moment nervously before sitting again and curling up into a ball next to his stereo.)*

WOLF. *(Flashing the grin again.)* So, I mean, I can pretend I didn't hear all that if it makes it easier?

JACK. No, I'm sorry. It's fine. He's just a little, I dont know.

WOLF. I had a roommate once who liked to set things on fire.

JACK. What?

WOLF. Uh huh. Old toys, clothing, one time my bed.

JACK. You win.

WOLF. Nah, it's not a contest. But I did sleep with a fire extinguisher and hide all of the matches before I kicked him out. I'm just saying, I understand how hard it is to find people to live with in the city.

JACK. Yes.

WOLF. The city does strange things to people.

JACK. Right, the city.

WOLF. So you're crashing here, does that mean you don't have your own room?

JACK. Oh no, I have a bedroom; it's in the back.

WOLF. Hmm.

*(The men sit on the couch for a moment. **JACK** smiles and ignores the hint.)*

Okay. How 'bout another drink?

JACK. Absolutely.

WOLF. I don't want to drink you dry or anything.

JACK. We've got plenty. I'll get it.

*(**JACK** fixes another drink for **WOLF**.)*

Do you go to that bar much?

WOLF. *(With a chuckle…)* You ask a lot of questions.

JACK. I'm a curious person.

WOLF. Didn't anyone ever tell you that'll get you into trouble?

JACK. I'm not big on "rules." So do you go to that bar much?

WOLF. Well, I've never seen you there before.

JACK. Is that a yes?

WOLF. Ya' know, I don't know. I stay home until I don't know how to stay home anymore, until I start to kind of not know who I am anymore, and then I go to a bar. It sounds, well, I don't want to think about how [it sounds.]

JACK. [No, I completely] understand what you're saying.

*(**JACK** gives **WOLF** the drink.)*

Well, some anyway. I don't go out a lot. But when I do, once I get there, it doesn't look the same to me as it does to everyone else. So I try to see what everyone else does or at least how I imagine they do.

WOLF. Close enough. So then you're there, at the bar, and suddenly you remember all the ways you don't fit. Even with all these people around you, guys around you. And you just want it to be, I shouldn't say you, I should say I, I'm talking about me, and then all of the sudden I want it to be this animal thing. Easy. Instinctive. But it's not, it doesn't happen like that for me. It's complicated for some reason.

JACK. Yes.

WOLF. And then you drink, I drink. I mean me, I start drinking.

JACK. Right.

WOLF. A lot.

JACK. Okay.

WOLF. And then you're sitting there at closing time laughing a little more than you should with a guy that's a little drunker than you'd like and your'e a little less drunk than you need to be for the whole thing to click and then, in the worst kind of fuck you moment, the lights come on. This ever happen to you? The lights come on and he's looking at you and you're looking at him, and he's fine. He's a guy and he's fine. And with the sounds of everyone leaving, shuffling out the door, it becomes real all of the sudden. And you're just clear-headed enough somewhere in the back of your brain to quietly think, "Am I lonely enough to fuck this guy?"

JACK. Oh.

WOLF. And is he thinking the same thing, about you? What if he's sitting there thinking that same thing about you?

(He finally looks over at **JACK** *and realizes…)*

But, uh, you know I'm not talking about you, right?

JACK. Oh, I didn't think you were.

WOLF. Okay, good.

*(***WOLF*** finishes his second drink.* **BEN** *gets up and begins to enter the hallway again, but stops himself. He stands in the doorway of his room with his back to the audience, listening.)*

JACK. But…that's a really intense story to tell someone you just met.

WOLF. Ugh, I really wasn't, I'm so bad at this. I didn't use to be bad at this, I mean I was never good at it, but I wasn't [this bad.]

JACK. [No, no, it's] fine. And, and maybe it wasn't intense so much as just…sad. Kind of really, deeply sad. I don't know, I didn't expect that from you.

*(**WOLF** laughs to himself.)*

WOLF. No?

JACK. Because you're really, because of how you look. Ya' know, good.

*(**WOLF** grins.)*

I think there's probably a way to tell basically that same story where it seems more exciting and a little less bleak.

WOLF. Ya' think?

JACK. Yep.

WOLF. I guess I don't know how to tell it that way anymore.

JACK. See, that's kind of a sad thing to say, too.

WOLF. Maybe you can cheer me up.

JACK. You're actually pretty sweet, aren't you?

WOLF. If you say so.

*(**WOLF** smiles and gently kisses **JACK**. It's intimate and very sweet. It's real. **BEN** lets out a frustrated sound and returns to being balled up by the stereo.)*

*(The **NARRATOR** claps once, interrupting and freezing the scene in tableau.)*

NARRATOR. That's nice, isn't it?

(She smiles and takes in the scene.)

It feels like stories, most stories, some stories, it feels like they often gloss over the lovely little things, doesn't it? The tiny moments that make everything else around them just melt away. Like a kiss. Like a "sweet" kiss. And stories can move so quickly, sometimes they don't afford the chance to linger. Hmmm.

(She lingers over the sight of the men.)

I should say that it's not a lovely moment for everyone though. I'll tell you that in the very same moment, lovely or not, Ben's heart was racing so fast. Not just fast, but hard. So hard that you might be able to hear it slamming around in his chest from there. Filling up his throat, deafening his ears with rushing blood. He was hiding in his room terrified by even the idea of what might be happening in the living room. Meanwhile, in the actual living room, well, these two had hearts pounding and blood rushing for an entirely different reason.

(Everything begins moving again. The men pull apart, both smiling.)

JACK. That was…

(WOLF laughs.)

WOLF. What? Unexpected, amazing, awful, aww come on, it was pretty great, right?

JACK. Sure.

WOLF. Yes it was.

JACK. I didn't think youd be so nice.

WOLF. Nice. Right. Good nice or bad nice?

JACK. No, I mean, you're actually… I like you.

WOLF. I like you too.

JACK. Really?

WOLF. Yes.

*(He takes **JACK**'s hand and presses it into his crotch. For a split second, **JACK** registers excitement and then, just as quickly, he nervously laughs off the moment pulling his hand away.)*

Huh, okay, you gotta help me out here, what, what was your name again?

JACK. Jack.

WOLF. Jack, right, you gotta' help me out here, Jack. Because I'm getting, I don't know, mixed signals.

I mean, the "roommate" thing aside, because we talked about how roommates are hard and all that, I'm sitting here and I'm into you and then we had a moment and I'm thinking green light and then there's this non-moment. I don't really, should I just leave?

(**JACK** *looks over his shoulder at* **BEN**'s *room, and gets a bit louder.*)

JACK. We're, we're having a good time, right?

(**WOLF** *snaps at him rapidly a few times to get his attention back.*)

WOLF. I'm over here. Is this some kind of weird thing with you and your [roommate?]

(**JACK** *quickly looks back to him.*)

JACK. [No, no, I'm] just being, trying to prove a point to him, that's not important. But part of me, part of me thought youd be more…

WOLF. It's cool, what? You thought I'd be more…?

JACK. Threatening.

WOLF. Huh.

JACK. Or dangerous.

WOLF. And that's why you [brought…?]

JACK. [Maybe.] I don't [know.]

WOLF. [Okay, so] we're not, I mean I thought we were connecting a little bit. But you were thinkin' [something else?]

JACK. [No, like you] said, unexpected.

WOLF. Because you expected me to be, I don't know, do I look scary? Is that what you're sayin', is that what you meant when you said "good?' Good as in scary?

JACK. No, I [just…]

WOLF. ['Cause,] I mean, that was the nicest thing anyone's said to me in a long time, a really long time, if you actually meant "good." But if you meant something else, well, that's less nice.

JACK. I meant good.

WOLF. Huh, I'm gonna go.

JACK. You don't have to, [seriously.]

WOLF. [Whatever.]

JACK. Please [stay.]

WOLF. [Honestly,] man, I don't really want to go either. I don't particularly like it out there and I don't wanna' go back to that bar and I don't wanna' go home alone, again.

JACK. Good, you don't have to; you're here.

WOLF. Look, I don't know if I can be the guy [you were…]

JACK. [Don't think] of it like that.

WOLF. So just, what does that mean? Threatening?

JACK. Forget it. We can just, it can be sweet.

WOLF. Convincing.

JACK. I don't know, just…stay.

WOLF. I like you, man, but this isn't really my kind of…

> (**WOLF** *looks at* **JACK**. *He takes a deep breath and makes the decision.*)

All right, ya' know…

> (*He moves in, kissing him hard. He throws* **JACK** *onto the couch, roughly, strips off his own shirt and climbs on top of* **JACK** *while speaking. He's smiling but it's less playful; it's aggressive.* **JACK** *is completely blindsided.*)

JACK. What are [you doing?]

WOLF. [So, fine, so] you need it to be a little rough, a little scary, okay. Okay, sure, I guess I can [do that.]

JACK. [I don't] know, I [wasn't…]

WOLF. [I'd rather] just, ya' know, I was diggin' the sweet thing, I thought that was kinda special, but I guess I can be whatever gets you off.

JACK. You don't [have to…]

WOLF. [This could] be fun, right?

JACK. Look, there's no [reason to....]

WOLF. [Shut-up.]

JACK. What?

> (WOLF *smacks* JACK *across the face.* JACK *is in shock.* BEN *is up in his room, on his feet and moving to his bedroom door to listen.*)

Don't do [that.]

> (*But he doesn't really mean it. And* WOLF *sees it.*)

WOLF. [You] like it?

JACK. Stop.

WOLF. (*with a growl...*) Aw, I can see you now, why couldn't I see you? Look at you. You like it.

JACK. No, I...

> (WOLF *hits him again. It is still. The men are breathing heavy.* WOLF *flinches towards* JACK *as if he might hit him again.* JACK *pulls away from him a bit.*)

> (WOLF *kisses* JACK *hard. He pulls away. Before he can get very far,* JACK *pulls him down and they are entwined on the couch.* JACK*'s shirt is stripped off and pants are yanked open in the ensuing desperate melee.*)

> (BEN *enters from his room. He watches the men. He looks to the* NARRATOR. *She shakes her head and sighs, indicating the men with her hand.* BEN *looks for a moment as if he might cry. Then he looks as if he might explode. Breathing heavy, he looks around the room, walks over to the woodpile, picks up the axe, and walks back to the couch.* WOLF *is still on top of* JACK, *his bare back exposed. With a cry that is part rage and part injured animal,* BEN *pulls the axe behind his head.* JACK *sees* BEN *and as* WOLF *begins to turn at the sound and* BEN *begins to bring the axe down on him.*)

> (*The* NARRATOR *claps once, interrupting and freezing the scene in tableau. She crosses to* BEN, *smiling, acknowledging the audience. She touches his face.*)

NARRATOR. You are very brave.

BEN. What am I doing?

NARRATOR. Jack might have been killed.

BEN. Been killed.

NARRATOR. By the wolf.

BEN. By the wolf.

NARRATOR. The wolf.

BEN. Yes.

NARRATOR. And you have to keep him safe.

BEN. I have to keep us safe.

NARRATOR. Safe and sound. Now take a deep breath and…

(She leans in whispering again. Light isolates **BEN** *as he seizes up and his eyes go wide. He clutches the axe tightly, his grip like steel.)*

(The **NARRATOR** *returns to her stool and* **JACK** *&* **WOLF** *drift away as the flood of language begins again. He lets the axe fall to his side, holding it near the end of the handle with the axe head on the floor. He periodically pounds the axe head into the floor as he speaks but is otherwise stark still.)*

BEN. The wood in my grip, the handle, wooden, thick, strong, tight, I feel it, the grain against my palm as I bring it down over and over and over, rubbing against my palms. No resistance, not going down, going into his back, easy, freshly sharpened blade cleaving, harder to pull it back, it wants to stick, but I do pull it back, again and again, then face wet. Red. Wet. Howling, yowling, then screaming, not me, not me, I don't scream. He screams while I grunt, exhaling everything inside out with each blow and it isn't fast, it feels like forever. It feels like forever. It feels like forever and I'm crying, not crying, my face is wet. And then it stops, all at once.

(Pause. His breathing is heavy, loud, an effort.)

I stop and I look.

(He drops the axe without even realizing it; he just releases it to the floor, a reflex upon seeing something truly awful.)

But I can't see the dead animal. I don't, won't see him. It's too dark, the dark is inside now, in here where it's supposed to be safe, sound, safe, the dark from out there, the forest, inside him, hiding, I let it out, cut it out, over and over and it's in here now, climbing out of his back, spilling out of him, red ribbons of, thick puddles on the floor, everything inside outside, everything outside in here, what did I do? And it has this smell, this scent, wet and heavy, raw, so strong, others will come, the smell is so strong. Have to think, have to be quiet, smart about, quiet, so, so quiet now, have to hide him, have to hide him, have to…

(As he reaches the end of the passage, lights fade on **BEN** *as the distant sounds of howling wind in a vast emptiness rise to consume him. The* **NARRATOR** *remains illuminated dimly along with the lava lamp as lights shift into…)*

IV. Deeper Into The Forest

NARRATOR. Eventually Jack stopped screaming. It may have been only a matter of moments, but it seemed like a very long time. In fact, he screamed so loud for so long that Ben had to press his hand over Jack's mouth to quiet him down, press his body over Jack's to still him. And he held Jack there until an awful, hollow stillness took over. Short breaths. Shallow. Barely even a sound. Eyes closed.

(She retrieves the bucket from next to her stool and crosses into the space while speaking. As she does, lights up on the space to reveal **WOLF** *sprawled out on the floor in front of the couch like a body that was simply left there.* **BEN** *and* **JACK** *are gone.)*

Now then, I did tell you back at the beginning that this wouldn't be pretty. So remember that, all right? And I mean, there's been an axe up here this whole time, which you probably noticed. Which isn't to say it's your fault if you didn't expect things to take a turn for the worse. I certainly could have been more specific.

(She pours the contents of the bucket onto **WOLF,** *all over his back and neck, and then splashes the remnants onto the couch and floor. It is blood and immediately transforms the space into a scene of extreme violence. She examines this and then replaces the bucket while speaking.)*

But here we are now. Rolling right along. Later in that same evening. Later in that same, long, dark evening…

(She looks at **WOLF.***)*

Oh, I should just…

(The **NARRATOR** *crosses over to* **WOLF** *and taps his shoulder. No reaction. She shakes his shoulder a bit harder. Nothing. She slaps his back, hard, and he jerks to life.)*

WOLF. Ugh. Ow. Holy shit that hurt.

NARRATOR. Come on, up you go.

WOLF. Just gimme' a minute.

(She helps him to his feet and might, to her distaste, get some blood on her hands. He stretches out his arms a bit, rolling out his neck.)

NARRATOR. Let's just get you over to the side.

WOLF. I'm a little dizzy.

NARRATOR. Well, you lost a lot of blood.

WOLF. Wait, what?

NARRATOR. Come on, come on.

*(After she leads him over to her stool and sits him down, she stands next to him, leaning against the wall. If she got blood on her hands, she might nonchalantly wipe them on **WOLF**'s jeans. They both face the apartment.)*

WOLF. What happened?

NARRATOR. Ah, he killed you.

WOLF. Oh, come on.

NARRATOR. With an axe.

WOLF. What the fuck? Why?

NARRATOR. You're a wolf.

WOLF. No, I'm not.

NARRATOR. You could argue, and I'd listen, that it was a game gone too far. That would be completely valid.

WOLF. Thank you.

NARRATOR. But for all intents and purposes you're a wolf. You were a wolf to Ben anyway. He was the roommate? You only met him for a minute.

WOLF. The awkward guy?

NARRATOR. He was afraid.

WOLF. The awkward guy killed me with an axe?

NARRATOR. You were something of a, have you ever heard the term tipping point?

WOLF. No.

NARRATOR. Shame.

WOLF. I should have stayed home tonight.

NARRATOR. It's really not fair.

WOLF. I was just lonely.

NARRATOR. Mmm, not fair at all. And I want you to know that you have my sympathies. Really. Even though I have to keep things moving along. In fact, they're both back there now…cutting up your body.

WOLF. What?!

NARRATOR. Mm hm, sure, there's plastic all over Jack's bedroom floor, a real mess. They're cutting it up to get rid of it, so it won't be found.

WOLF. Stop saying "it," you're talking about my body.

NARRATOR. They're afraid of the other wolves coming.

WOLF. I'm not a fucking wolf!

NARRATOR. I can absolutely see how it's a really unfortunate misunderstanding.

WOLF. You know what, that's kind of a huge fucking understatement, okay. Can you just give me a minute?

NARRATOR. Sure.

(The **NARRATOR** *sways back and forth for a moment while* **WOLF** *stews. It's only a brief moment though and then, after some thought, he bites his fist and cries out from the pain. It might even bleed a bit.)*

WOLF. Fuck!

NARRATOR. Why would you do that?

WOLF. To wake up.

NARRATOR. You'd do better to start accepting what happened. And if you ask me, and you didn't, but if you did ask then I'd say you maybe got the better end of the deal.

WOLF. Apparently, I was repeatedly struck with an axe.

NARRATOR. But you didn't know that until I told you. And look at you now, you're fine.

WOLF. I'm not fine; I'm dead.

NARRATOR. It doesn't hurt though, does it?

WOLF. My hand does.

NARRATOR. You bit yourself.

WOLF. They're cutting up my body!

NARRATOR. Actually, Ben is doing most of the work; the actual cutting. The labor-intensive stuff, the real stomach churning kind of, well, you get the idea.

WOLF. This is so fucked up.

NARRATOR. I think Jack actually liked you. He's crying. I don't know if that helps at all?

WOLF. Not really.

NARRATOR. Ah. Well, he's pretty worthless in the end, when it comes to anything emotionally difficult. Immature. Maybe. You really dodged a bullet with that one.

WOLF. Ya think?

NARRATOR. Yes, well, anyway Ben made Jack do the teeth; smash the teeth.

(**WOLF** *rubs his mouth, disappointed.*)

WOLF. Aww, not the teeth.

NARRATOR. With a hammer.

WOLF. Ugh.

NARRATOR. It hurts just to think about, doesn't it?

WOLF. And I had such a great smile.

NARRATOR. You should have smiled more. That's my observation.

WOLF. Maybe. I guess that's fair.

NARRATOR. Mm hm.

WOLF. But when I did smile, I mean, it was good.

(*He smiles at her. She gently touches his face with a grin.*)

NARRATOR. Yes, it was. But Ben has a thing about teeth; they make him uncomfortable. So Jack had to do that part. And they've never done this before, disposed of a body, in case you were wondering. You're the first.

WOLF. Great.

(She crosses over, picks up the axe and rubs it on the couch a bit. Ensuring that the head is bloody.)

NARRATOR. So I'm sure it's a much more in depth disposal of the evidence than it really needs to be. Fueled by paranoia or guilt or fear? Take your pick.

WOLF. I can sort of feel it, feel him cutting me up.

NARRATOR. Mmm.

WOLF. But like it's far away.

NARRATOR. You're not that dead yet. Fresh kill.

WOLF. "Fresh kill."

NARRATOR. Fresh kill.

WOLF. "Fresh kill, fresh kill," my mouth feels empty, my whole body.

NARRATOR. No teeth. No you.

*(**WOLF** cocks his head, aware of something…)*

WOLF. They're done. Cutting me up. I can feel from here that they're done.

*(The **NARRATOR** examines the axe and, satisfied, replaces the axe where it was dropped and moves quickly to stand beside **WOLF** in her area of the stage.)*

NARRATOR. Quiet now, let's watch.

*(She points to the doorway in the back of the space. **BEN** and **JACK** enter slowly. **BEN** is in his white t-shirt and jeans, **JACK** still shirtless. Both of them are dragging large, black, garbage bags. Probably three in total, weighty and awkward. Both men are blood splattered and their hands and arms are wet with it. They look shell-shocked, but **BEN** is alert. He's getting things done. They try to speak in hushed tones, like they're hiding. But it's hard.)*

BEN. Just, just stop for a minute.

*(They stop. **BEN** wipes the hair off of his forehead with the back of his hand, smearing it red with blood.)*

BEN. *(cont.)* We can't take these outside until right before the trash pick-up.

JACK. You have blood on your face.

BEN. Let's put the bags in the bathroom for now.

JACK. Why?

BEN. Because I don't want to look at him right now, okay?

> *(**BEN** dumps the trash bags in the bathroom, all of them as **JACK** just stands there, no longer helping. **BEN** paces in the hall as **JACK** lingers in the hallway and stares at the trash bags.)*

WOLF. Are you, come on, that's me?

NARRATOR. You have to be quiet.

WOLF. I'm just supposed to sit here [and…]

> *(The **NARRATOR** slaps her hand over **WOLF**'s mouth.)*

NARRATOR. [Shhh.]

BEN. Stop looking at it.

> *(Pause. **BEN** goes to the kitchen, drinks a healthy amount directly from a liquor bottle and then heads back to the hallway.)*

I said stop looking at it.

JACK. No.

BEN. So, can I just ask, everything was gonna' be okay, I mean, stay, don't stay, it would have been fine, it would have hurt, but it would have been fine, what were you trying to prove?

JACK. You didn't have to cut him up.

BEN. You know what? Don't.

JACK. You didn't have to cut him up.

BEN. It's easier this way, to get rid of what's left.

JACK. You didn't have to cut [him up.]

BEN. [Stop saying] that, Jack, stop it. I'm taking care of things, of you, just let me do it and you have to pull it together. I don't know, but pull it together.

JACK. The bathroom looks smaller.

BEN. It's not.

JACK. The whole apartment looks smaller.

BEN. It's not.

JACK. Even my skin, my skin feels [smaller.]

BEN. [Stop it.]

JACK. What did you do?

BEN. What did "we" do?

JACK. No.

BEN. It's like you said; it's like hunting.

(**JACK** *finally looks up from the trash bags at* **BEN**.)

JACK. You…you really are completely insane.

BEN. You smashed his teeth with a hammer.

JACK. Oh god, I don't think I can handle this, I don't think I can see it but I saw it or do that and I did it anyway and I don't know what to do and he's all over my hands.

(**BEN** *looks annoyed.*)

BEN. It washes off.

JACK. He's in plastic bags.

BEN. It was self-defense.

JACK. He's in multiple plastic [bags.]

BEN. [He] attacked you.

JACK. He didn't. I liked, ugh, he was just a guy.

BEN. Don't say it like that, "he was just a guy." "A guy." He was a fucking wolf and this is what we do: we have to kill wolves before they kill us. It's a big city, forest, it's a big darkness and who knows what he would have done, what he would have taken, how he could have hurt you, no, it could have been really bad.

JACK. Could have been really [bad?]

BEN. [Yes.]

JACK. You killed some poor man that I [brought back….]

BEN. [We didn't] kill a man; we killed a wolf, that's important, that matters, we wouldn't kill a guy, [would we?]

JACK. [I didn't] kill anyone!

BEN. Don't yell! Don't yell. We have to be quiet. Now listen, you brought him here, you fucking brought a wolf into the only safe place we have so you sure as hell had a hand in this.

JACK. There's so much blood.

BEN. We'll clean it up.

JACK. I hate it.

BEN. I know.

JACK. I hate it.

BEN. *(With a snarl…)* Then fucking stop looking at it.

JACK. Ben. He wasn't really a wolf.

BEN. He was.

JACK. His name [was…]

BEN. [I don't want] to know.

JACK. He was nice.

(BEN explodes.)

BEN. Just, ugh, shut up, just shut the fuck up, you never listen, ever!!!

(He stops himself.)

He was a wolf, he was a wolf, that's what they do. They lie, they connive. They smile, but you can't look at the grin, you look at the teeth underneath, not at the warm eyes, but at the hunger behind them, the dark parts that they don't want you to see. You think he was nice? Or do you, you think he would have, what, loved you? You think an animal like that was capable of love? You think he [would have…?]

JACK. [Stop, Stop it!]

(Pause. BEN *puts a hand on* JACK*'s shoulder.* JACK *flinches away.)*

BEN. Please keep your voice down.

JACK. I wanted you to see it isn't dangerous.

BEN. It was dangerous.

JACK. He's the one who died!!

BEN. Shhh, we both need to be quiet now, Jack, okay? It's so important that we be quiet now.

JACK. Why?

*(Their conversation takes on an intense, confidential timbre. The **NARRATOR** and **WOLF** lean in to hear them.)*

BEN. In case there are others, in case they're listening.

JACK. Others? There are more?

BEN. Of course there are more, there are always more. Wolves travel [in packs.]

JACK. [And they're] coming here?

BEN. I don't know, they might. They might have tracked you two, from the bar, through the forest; they might still track [you here.]

JACK. [You're trying] to scare me on purpose, you're [trying to…]

BEN. [I wouldn't] do that, but I'm not going to lie to you. It's awful out there and it came in here, the wolves are out there and one came in here. He's in those bags because he came in here.

JACK. Yes.

BEN. And if one came here, no matter why, then others might follow him.

JACK. How?

BEN. The screaming.

JACK. Oh god.

BEN. The smell.

JACK. It's awful.

BEN. They can follow it.

JACK. The wolves?

BEN. They can follow it to us.

JACK. The wolves.

BEN. Yes.

(Pause. Then **JACK** *comes undone. Full tilt undone.)*

JACK. I saw it, I saw it, Ben, I didn't want to see it, but it was like I could hear you in my head and then I saw it, that bar was full of them, eyes dancing, tongues over teeth, I always see it, I've tried so hard, but I always see it, wanting, so many of them climbing over one and another, hungry, and the streets on the way home, thick with their breath and the sound [of their…]

BEN. [Shhh.]

JACK. What are we gonna' do?

BEN. If they do come here [to…]

JACK. [They] will come here. You just said [they will!]

BEN. [If that] happens, [then…]

JACK. [Yes.]

BEN. We have to hide.

JACK. That's a good plan, that's a, how can we hide from them?

BEN. You'll just be very careful, [like me.]

JACK. [No! No, if they come] in here, you said if he came here then others would find us, where can we hide in this tiny fucking apartment if it's overrun by [wolves?]

BEN. [No, it's] not going [to be…]

JACK. [You said,] you said that, if it's out there and [comes in here…]

BEN. [I know what I] said, Jack, just let me think [for a…!]

JACK. [You don't have] any idea, do you?! Oh my god, you're supposed [to know…]

BEN. [Calm down!]

JACK. *(With an awful laugh.)* Calm down?!

BEN. You can't panic; that's when you start to make mistakes.

JACK. No, that's when you start to make mistakes, Ben. I'm finally thinking clearly. We're going to be overrun [by wolves.]

*(**JACK** starts to push the couch towards the front door.)*

BEN. [What are] you doing?!

JACK. We have to block the door, make it harder for them to get in, it might buy [us some time!]

BEN. [Making all] of this noise only brings them here faster!

JACK. Do you think it makes a difference now?!

BEN. I don't know, [but we…!]

JACK. [We killed one] of them and now we're going to be gutted!!

(*The* **NARRATOR** *claps once, interrupting and freezing the scene in tableau. As she speaks, she crosses to* **BEN***, smiling, acknowledging the audience.*)

WOLF. Oh my god, what the fuck is wrong with these guys?

NARRATOR. Just a second, Wolf.

WOLF. Please stop calling me that.

NARRATOR. It's what you are now.

WOLF. It's not what I am; I was a lonely guy who thought he was gonna have sex and now I'm a dead body in pieces in plastic fucking bags.

NARRATOR. Fine. It's who you are now.

WOLF. How is that distinction any better?

NARRATOR. And I'm keeping Ben's story moving, that's who I am.

WOLF. Maybe it doesn't need to keep moving, you ever think of that? Fucked up little psycho.

NARRATOR. I can certainly understand how you might feel that way.

WOLF. Good.

NARRATOR. I sympathize, like I mentioned.

WOLF. Great!

NARRATOR. That doesn't mean I'll stop.

WOLF. Fuck you.

NARRATOR. I already conceded that its not fair, but please be patient.

WOLF. That's rich. That's really amazingly fucked [up.]

NARRATOR. [Because] Wolf, and that's the role you're playing now, becoming, even if you just used to be a sad man at a bar who didn't smile enough. This wasn't supposed to happen. I mean, in the story it happens, but neither of them meant for it to go this far. And they're not heartless; I should tell you that.

WOLF. I don't [think that's…]

(She holds up her hand.)

NARRATOR. [Ah, ah. You] might not want to hear it, trust me, I know. But they're really not. So they'll regret it. And that regret will have a form, a face. And that means you stick around.

WOLF. To watch them?

NARRATOR. To haunt them.

WOLF. So I don't get laid, I do get axed to death and cut into pieces, and now I'm a ghost?

NARRATOR. Look, I can see how you may not like me, [but if…]

WOLF. [At all.]

NARRATOR. At all. But you clearly don't understand your role yet and if you ever want to actually do anything with all of that anger and frustration, then you'll sit there and you'll watch. Quietly.

WOLF. There better be a pay off.

NARRATOR. It's not like you have any other options.

(He crosses his arms in surrender and settles in to watch. She leans in with care and whispers something in his ear, blocking her mouth with her hand. Again, it is a private thing.)

*(**BEN** suddenly shrugs her away.)*

BEN. *(quietly…)* No.

NARRATOR. What?

BEN. I don't want to hear anything else.

NARRATOR. Don't be silly. I'm helping.

BEN. I killed one wolf, I can kill the rest. By myself.

NARRATOR. This is the [very thing…]

BEN. [I don't need] you to tell me anything.

NARRATOR. Ben, I'm managing a lot here, it's not the time to [lose your…]

BEN. [You're a] liar!!!

*(Pause. The **NARRATOR** glances at the audience, embarrassed, then back to **BEN** with a new intensity.)*

NARRATOR. I'm doing my very best to give you [what you….]

BEN. [Safe and] sound, you said that. Safe and sound.

NARRATOR. Until you start to think it's not. But I can help [you if…]

BEN. [I had to] dismember a body.

NARRATOR. You chose to dismember a body.

BEN. No, you said, warm and wet, you said to [hide the…]

NARRATOR. [You said] those things.

BEN. No, no, in my ear, spilling out of his back, it feels like forever, [you said…]

NARRATOR. [There is] always a dark and awful part before you reach the [other side.]

BEN. [Ugh, I] can do it myself.

NARRATOR. You think so?

BEN. It's Jack and me now. Jack and me. It's the two of us against that awful, against these wolves. Just the two of us.

NARRATOR. You don't have Jack. You broke Jack. Look at him; he's broken. And Wolf is over there ready to explode.

WOLF. *(with a snarl)* Yes, he really fucking is.

NARRATOR. Be quiet. Now, Ben, pushing me away won't get you what you want. You need to listen because you have no idea how quickly things can get very dark in this very [small apartment.]

BEN. [I'm covered] in blood.

NARRATOR. Darker and darker.

BEN. No.

NARRATOR. Smaller and smaller.

BEN. Don't do that, don't threaten me.

NARRATOR. It's not a threat.

BEN. It keeps getting worse and worse, your voice like glass in my head, jagged glass and clanging bells. This isn't what I wanted, blood [everywhere.]

NARRATOR. [Ben, this] isn't my fault.

BEN. Then whose fault is it?

NARRATOR. Yours.

BEN. Okay, okay, fine, then I want the story where love triumphs or good wins or the woodsman kills the wolf and saves the [day and…]

NARRATOR. [That's just] a nicer version of this.

BEN. Yes!

NARRATOR. Well, that's not your story.

BEN. I can make it my story, I don't need you [for that]

NARRATOR. [I'm the one who] keeps this all from just [swallowing you up.]

BEN. [I'm not listening] to you [anymore, none of it]

NARRATOR. [It won't] get better without me.

BEN. It can't get any worse.

NARRATOR. Yes, it can.

> (BEN *pounds the axe handle into the floor causing the* NARRATOR *to flinch. He suddenly seizes up as his eyes go wide, he's starting the next chapter on his own. He clutches the axe tightly. The* NARRATOR *backs away from* BEN *as the words begin spilling out, the now familiar flood of language, religious in its fervor, a loss of control. The* NARRATOR *seems shocked as the scene begins to move again without her; she's supposed to be in charge of this kind of thing. The lights begin to isolate* BEN *as he moves on with the story without her.*)

BEN. You get used to it, you have to get used to it, have to, because everything's always fading, dimming, getting [darker...]

NARRATOR. [Ben, this] isn't [very wise.]

BEN. [Dimming,] everything's always darker, the city becomes a forest becomes a nightmare and bangs on the door, bangs, comes through the door, shaking the floor, the body comes apart, cut apart, wet pieces, fur, teeth, blood [inside the...]

(She begins backing toward her stool.)

NARRATOR. [Once you go down] [this road, it'll go fast]

BEN. [Inside the smallest place to] hide in the largest city, forest, city, forest, the horrible things that fill that dark. I can kill them, will kill them, the horrible things that, a happy ending, horrible things. Kill them.

(He pulls back and slams the axe into the floor.)

Kill them.

NARRATOR. Fine.

(He pulls back and slams the axe into the floor.)

BEN. Kill...them.

*(He kneels down, leaning on the axe. The lights return to a dim wash as the distant sounds of howling wind in a vast emptiness rise to consume him. The **NARRATOR** walks back to her area and stares **BEN** down as lights shift into...)*

V. Biting The Hand That Feeds You

NARRATOR. All right. Only moments later, with Ben still breathing heavy and Jack still in a bewildered kind of shock. The two men found the very small apartment getting darker and darker as the bags holding the dismembered body of the dead wolf sat very still in [the bathroom.]

BEN. [I told you to] stop it!

*(The **NARRATOR** is not pleased as she sits down on her stool.)*

Jack?

*(Suddenly **JACK** is in motion again, picking up from the moment he froze.)*

JACK. I don't want them to kill us!!

BEN. Jack, I'm in control now, I'm ready.

JACK. Ready?!

*(**JACK** has to look around for **BEN**, who is now in a different place post-freeze and somehow has the axe again.)*

BEN. We can't keep them out now, couch against the door, even if we stack everything in this apartment against the door, they're coming. But I can fight them. Just look at me.

(He stands up, eyes wide, smiling, holding the axe out in one hand.)

I'll protect you.

JACK. Against all of them.

BEN. *(laughing)* I'm the hero in the story now.

WOLF. What the fuck?

BEN. And we get a happy ending, Jack.

JACK. Why?

BEN. Because I love you.

JACK. Why?

(**BEN** *kisses* **JACK.** *He pushes* **BEN** *away abruptly and covers his mouth.*)

I think I'm gonna' be sick.

(*He stumbles into the bathroom and kneels down falls down, but he doesn't actually get sick.* **BEN** *crosses into the living room.* **WOLF** *begins to get anxious on the stool shaking his head back and forth with disgust at the sight of* **BEN** *with the axe.*)

WOLF. I thought you were in charge of this freak show?

NARRATOR. I am.

(**BEN** *looks directly at the* **NARRATOR** *as he calls out to* **JACK.**)

BEN. Everything's gonna be okay now, Jack.

NARRATOR. Huh. All right, then.

BEN. I will keep us safe and sound.

(*The* **NARRATOR** *leans forward on her stool…*)

NARRATOR. Just remember you asked for it.

(**BEN** *crosses away to the bathroom doorway.*)

JACK. All of this blood.

BEN. Are you sick?

JACK. I don't know.

BEN. We are going to be fine.

JACK. I could taste it on your lips.

(**BEN** *rubs* **JACK**'*s back and tries to comfort him. The* **NARRATOR** *calls out to* **WOLF** *almost sing-songy…*)

NARRATOR. Oh, Wolf.

WOLF. This is so fucking wrong.

NARRATOR. I agree.

WOLF. He doesn't get to be the hero.

NARRATOR. So then say it louder.

WOLF. You told me to stay [quiet.]

NARRATOR. [Change] in plan. Darker quicker. Again. Louder.

WOLF. He doesn't get to be the hero!

NARRATOR. Louder, please.

> *(**WOLF** screams. It is full of rage, full of wrath. It is a roar. It swallows the space. The lights pulse up with a flicker then return to a dimmer level, even a bit darker now.)*

> *(**JACK** cowers in the bathroom. **BEN** rushes into the bathroom and crouches next to him, clutching the axe defensively. **WOLF** looks at the **NARRATOR**, eyes wide. She crosses her arms.)*

WOLF. They can, they can hear me?

NARRATOR. Like a very bad memory.

WOLF. A very bad memory.

NARRATOR. That's what I said.

WOLF. That haunts them.

NARRATOR. And now your patience will start to pay off.

WOLF. Haunts them.

> *(She bends down and begins to pull the edge of the white tape that marks the frontdoor up. She hands the end of it to **WOLF**.)*

NARRATOR. And there are all kinds of ways to do that.

> *(**WOLF**'s smile returns, only somehow twisted now, more animal.)*

WOLF. Why are you helping me?

NARRATOR. Don't think of it like that.

WOLF. I wanna know why.

NARRATOR. This is the story Ben wants. Even if it won't go well for him.

WOLF. *(Almost a growl…)* It's not going to go well for him.

NARRATOR. That's… unfortunate.

> *(As the **NARRATOR** continues speaking, **WOLF** begins tearing up the tape from the floor. The rooms slowly disappear. The entire world slowly disappears, as he*

pulls up more and more, winding his way ever closer to the two men cowering in the bathroom.)

(He slowly drifts from a hunched over figure pulling up tape to an animal tearing through the space.)

(He stops when the only tape left is the small box that demarcates the bathroom, currently filled with **BEN**, **JACK** *and the garbage bags. He flips over the bed, knocks the couch over, scatters books and wood across the space.)*

Once upon a time there were two young men, Ben and Jack, who were once in love and then in some other kind of thing, something like need. And then they did something so awful that they were never able to look each other in the eye again.

(She indicates **BEN** *and* **JACK**.*)*

But it was so dark that they couldn't see each other anyway. Maybe.

BEN. *(Quietly.)* Help.

NARRATOR. And he was the hero.

*(***WOLF** *snarls at them from the dark.* **BEN** *drops the axe and he and* **JACK** *huddle together in the bathroom next to the trash bags.)*

Just like he wanted. But it's easy to be brave right up until the moment your world starts to come undone. It's easy to make proclamations about courage right up to the moment that you need to be courageous.

BEN. Help, please.

(She looks over her shoulder at **BEN**.*)*

NARRATOR. So maybe, just maybe, there is a kind of moral to all of this.

BEN. I need you.

JACK. Shhh.

NARRATOR. Which is a shame, because I used to so love when we would sing together.

BEN. I was wrong.

JACK. *(very quiet…)* I can hear him.

BEN. I was wrong; I [love you.]

JACK. [Shhh, be] quiet.

BEN. I'm so sorry.

NARRATOR. Sometimes people just don't know what to do when confronted with the world. Not the idea of it, the actual thing. And sometimes people don't know that they're those people until it's too late to be anything else. Because after all…

(As he closes in on the bathroom, **WOLF** *roars at the men, causing the lights to flicker. The men cling to each other.)*

It is a very big, very scary place out there.

*(***WOLF*** *crouches down on his haunches, hands full of tape on the floor in front of him for balance. He stares at the men, panting from the effort of destroying their apartment. His breathing is savage and animal.)*

(She crouches down and rubs her finger on the floor, then lifts her hand rolling the wet blood between her fingers.)

But Ben never sang much after that night. And Jack never laughed much after that night. Ever. And the memory of their encounter with the wolf taunted them, haunted them, playing tricks with their eyes, their ears, with the secret parts of their brains. Together. Alone. In a very small apartment in a very large city. Always with the wolf at the door.

(She glances back. **WOLF** *scratches on the floor. The men cringe in fear.)* And their hearts beat so fast.

*(***WOLF*** *scratches the floor. The* **NARRATOR** *looks away.)*

And their hearts beat. So. Fast.

*(***WOLF***'s heavy breathing is the only sound as he looms near them. The men cower. He roars again, even louder, causing the remaining light to flicker again. The men scream. Blackout.)*

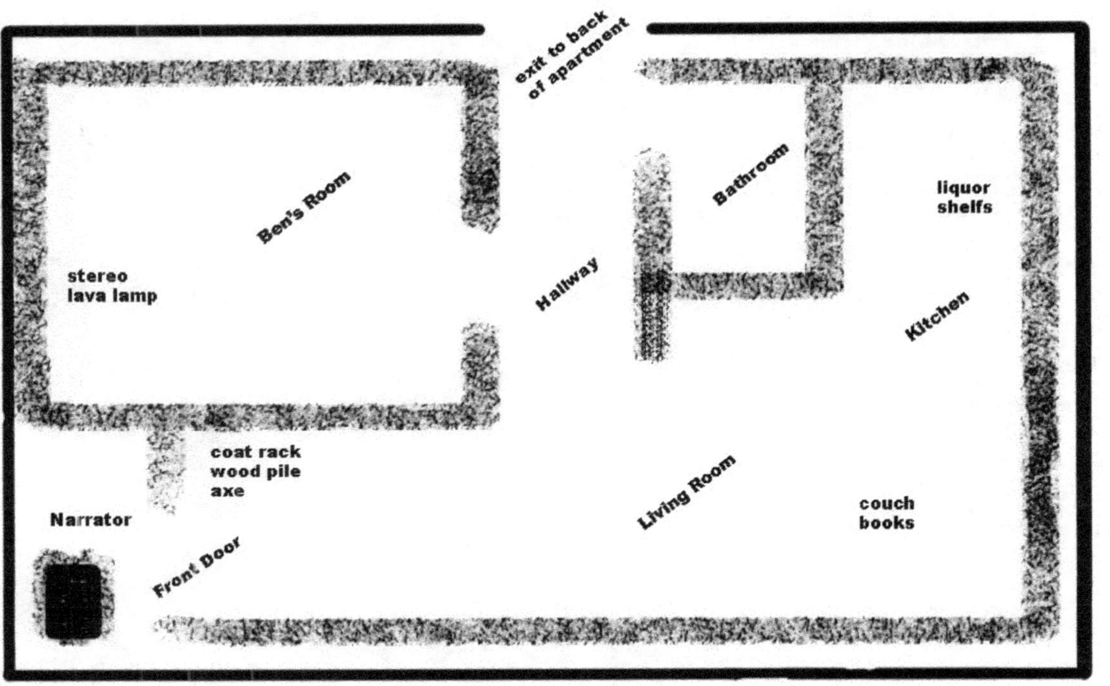

exit to back
of apartment
Ben's Room
stereo
lava lamp
Hallway
Bathroom
liquor
shelfs
Kitchen
coat rack
wood pile
axe
Living Room
couch
books
Narrator
Front Door